When They Are Up...

To Dan, who is always up for a challenge
Maggee and Richard

To Ann and Gail for getting me started
Kirsti

Fitzhenry & Whiteside Limited
195 Allstate Parkway, Markham, Ontario L3R 4T8

In the United States:
121 Harvard Avenue, Suite 2, Allston, Massachusetts 02134

www.fitzhenry.ca godwit@fitzhenry.ca

Fitzhenry & Whiteside acknowledges with thanks the Canada Council for the Arts, the Government of Canada through its Book Publishing Industry Development Program, and the Ontario Arts Council for their support of our publishing program.

National Library of Canada Cataloguing in Publication Data

Spicer, Maggee
When they are up / by Maggee Spicer and Richard Thompson; illustrations by Kirsti Anne Wakelin.

ISBN 1-55041-707-X (bound)—ISBN 1-55041-709-6 (pbk.)

I. Wakelin, Kirsti Anne II. Title.

PS8589.H53W48 2003 jC811'.54 C2003-902334-6
PZ7

U.S. Publisher Cataloging-in-Publication Data
(Library of Congress Standards)

Spicer, Maggee
When they are up / Maggee Spicer and Richard Thompson; [illustrated by] Kirsti Anne Wakelin. —1st ed.
[34] p. : col. ill. ; cm.
Summary: A delightful twist on a traditional nursery rhyme — The Grand old Duke of York has many soldiers eager to do his bidding. Although these soldiers have been trained to march, they have little discipline and no sense of decorum.
ISBN 1-55041-707-X
ISBN 1-55041-709-6 (pbk.)
1. Nursery rhymes, English _Juvenile literature. 2. Children's poetry. (1. Nursery rhymes. 2. Poetry.)
I. Wakelin, Kirsti Anne. II. Title.
398.8 21 PZ8.3.T566Wh 2004

Design by Wycliffe Smith Design Inc.
Printed in Hong Kong

When They Are Up...

BY MAGGEE SPICER
AND RICHARD THOMPSON

Illustrated by Kirsti Anne Wakelin

Fitzhenry & Whiteside

The Grand Old Duke of York,
He has ten thousand men.
He marches them up to the top of the hill
And he marches them down again.

And when they are up they are up.
And when they are down they are down.
And when they are only halfway up,
They are neither up nor down.

And when they are up they wear wigs.
And when they are down they wear boots.

And when they are only halfway up,
They dress in silly suits.

And when they are up they knit scarves.
And when they are down they knit socks.
And when they are only halfway up,
They knit overcoats for rocks.

And when they are up they all laugh.
And when they are down they all cry.
And when they are only halfway up,
They hit each other with pies.

RULES to PLAY BY
RULES to

And when they are up they all cheat.
And when they are down they play fair.
And when they are only halfway up,
They wrestle with grizzly bears.

The Grand Old Duke of York,
He has ten thousand men.
He marches them up to the top of the hill
And he marches them down again.

And I am not one. Oh no!
And you are not one. I'm glad!
But my brother has gone to be one of his men,
And my mom is awfully sad

Because...

When they are up they tell lies.
And when they are down they tell tales.
And when they are only halfway up,
They shop at rummage sales.

And when they are up they play chess.
And when they are down they play tag.

And when they are only halfway up,
They catch armadillos in bags.

RIP VAN WINKLE
5

And when they are up they read books.
And when they are down they write poems.
And when they are only halfway up,
They play basketball with gnomes.

And when they are up they eat soup.
And when they are down they eat cheese.

And when they are only halfway up,
They eat whatever they please.

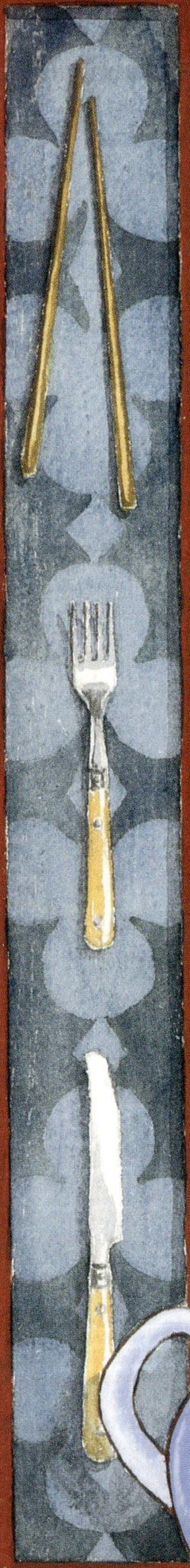

The Grand Old Duke of York,
He has ten thousand men.
He marches them up to the top of the hill
And he marches them down again.

And I am not one. Not me!
And you are not one. No way!
But my brother says it is lots of fun,
So my mom is joining today!

When They Are Up...

The Grand Old Duke of York,
He has ten thousand men.
He marches them up to the top of the hill
And he marches them down again.

And when they are up they are up.
And when they are down they are down.
And when they are only halfway up,
They are neither up nor down.

And when they are up they wear wigs.
And when they are down they wear boots.
And when they are only halfway up,
They dress in silly suits.

And when they are up they knit scarves.
And when they are down they knit socks.
And when they are only halfway up,
They knit overcoats for rocks.

And when they are up they all laugh.
And when they are down they all cry.
And when they are only halfway up,
They hit each other with pies.

And when they are up they all cheat.
And when they are down they play fair.
And when they are only halfway up,
They wrestle with grizzly bears.

The Grand Old Duke of York,
He has ten thousand men.
He marches them up to the top of the hill
And he marches them down again.

And I am not one. Oh no!
And you are not one. I'm glad!
But my brother has gone to be one of his men,
And my mom is awfully sad
Because...

When they are up they tell lies.
And when they are down they tell tales.
And when they are only halfway up,
They shop at rummage sales.

And when they are up they play chess.
And when they are down they play tag.
And when they are only halfway up,
They catch armadillos in bags.

And when they are up they read books.
And when they are down they write poems.
And when they are only halfway up,
They play basketball with gnomes.

And when they are up they eat soup.
And when they are down they eat cheese.
And when they are only halfway up,
They eat whatever they please.

The Grand Old Duke of York,
He has ten thousand men.
He marches them up to the top of the hill
And he marches them down again.

And I am not one. Not me!
And you are not one. No way!

But my brother says it is lots of fun,
So my mom is joining today!

What do the creators of this book do
when *they* are halfway up?

They dress in silly suits.

Maggee Spicer
as the Queen of Hearts

Richard Thompson
as the King of Hearts

Kirsti Anne Wakelin
as the Queen of Spades